SUNNY
the Sneaker

Written by Michele Christian-Oldham   Illustrated by Michele G. Katz

three
bean press

For Aaron, Emily and Sara—
No matter how old you are, I
will always love to hear the
pitter-patter of your feet.
I love you always,
Mom

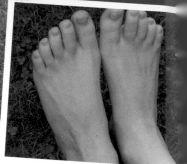

Aaron

Emily

Sara

Sunny the Sneaker
Published by:
Three Bean Press, LLC
P.O. Box 301711
Jamaica Plain, MA 02130
info@threebeanpress.com • www.threebeanpress.com

Publishers Cataloging-in-Publication Data
Christian-Oldham, Michele
Sunny the Sneaker / by Michele Christian-Oldham.
p. cm.
Summary: When Sunny the Sneaker's parents decide the time has come for him to be worn, he does a little "sole-searching." Sunny doesn't love sports, or even feet, which is a shame as he belongs to a sports-loving teen. This, along with a fun-loving dog and an active household, leaves Sunny shaking in his boots....

ISBN 978-0-9882212-7-7.
[1. Children—Fiction. 2. Young Readers—Fiction. 3. Sneakers—Fiction. 4. Humor—Fiction.] I. Katz, Michele G., Ill. II. Title.
LCCN 2013954466

Printed and bound in China by Guangzhou Yi Cai Printing, through Four Colour Print Group in November 2013. Batch J130725FC04

10 9 8 7 6 5 4 3 2 1

About the Author

Michele Christian-Oldham is a longtime writer who loves to pen funny and light-hearted stories, often using the antics of her son and twin girls for material. Michele lives in Massachusetts and has contributed to many newspapers as well as written short stories for well-known books including the popular *Chicken Soup for the Soul* series. She credits her warmth and creativity to her children, family and, quite possibly, to the fact that she is a left-handed redhead. An Army wife, Michele has undoubtedly seen her share of the serious, but through her work and attitude she champions that "life can be fun and games, too!" Visit www.michelechristianoldham.com to learn more.

About the Illustrator

Michele Katz started making "books" by stapling pieces of paper together and drawing on the pages at the ripe old age of six. By the time she was in middle school, she had decided on Syracuse University for her BFA in illustration. (Fortunately the school approved of her choice!) Since then, Michele has been creating whimsical art designed to make people smile. Her work has appeared in numerous magazines and on a range of different products from t-shirts to yoga mats. She also designs greeting cards and is the illustrator of *The Quilt Book*, written by Diane C. Ohanesian. She currently resides in Rhode Island. You can see more of her works at www.creationsbymit.com

Ever since I was a baby
sneaker, I lived in the
musty hall
closet of the
Fuller family
home.

My mother was a beautiful, bright yellow tennis shoe, and my father was a sporty, orange high-top. I wish I could tell you that I inherited my parents' athleticism—I didn't. But I did inherit their cheerful appearance, so they felt that it was appropriate to name me Sunny. I am Sunny the Sneaker!

My first real taste for adventure began when my parents decided I was old enough to face the Fuller home on my own. I would belong to the Fuller's 14-year-old son, Nate, who, unlike me, loved to play sports.

The closet door was cracked open bit, allowing me to peek out beyond the shadows of the parkas and raincoats and into the sunlit hallway. I nervously waved good-bye to my parents with my shoelace, wondering if I could do this alone. But I was a big sneaker now. It was time to be worn, and Mom and Dad felt Nate would be the perfect fit for me.

The thought of being on my own sent shivers down to my toes, but I quickly realized that I wasn't alone—which was scarier still. I spied two nickel-sized lights glowing back at me, and they were slowly coming closer. They looked more like eyes—eager eyes, waiting and ready to leap on an unsuspecting small object—like me. It was the Fuller's dog, Max. I cowered in the closet, hoping he wouldn't notice me, but in a flash he came bounding toward me. He skidded to a stop in front of the closet door, pushing it open with his nose to reach me. He sniffed me wildly. His cold, wet nose tickled. I begged for him to stop, yet I couldn't stop giggling. He playfully picked me up in his mouth.

OH, WHAT STINKY BREATH!

Max ran downstairs with me clamped in his canines, out the front pet door and began to frolic in a nearby mud puddle. He threw me up in the air and let me free-fall right into the brown pool of muck. SPLASH! Cool mud seeped into my fresh canvas skin.

"PLEASE STOP!" I shouted at Max, but he kept right on playing, mocking me with the delighted wag of his tail.

Eventually, Max grew tired of the game. He carried me over to a shady oak tree in the front yard and lay down to rest. He snuggled me in the crook of his neck. His fur was soft like a blanket, and the warm air felt good on my skin, drying out the wet mud. I was sleepy and dozed off under the tree with Max.

I must have slept very soundly, because when I awoke, it was morning, and I was in the upstairs bathroom. The house was very quiet.

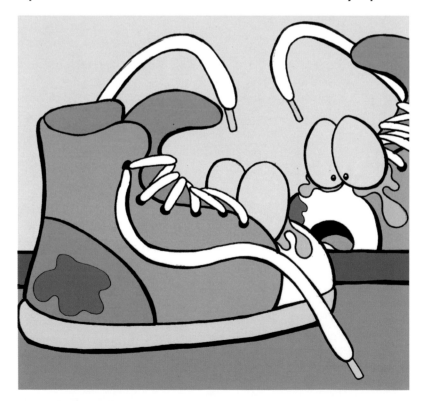

I looked at my dried mud–splattered body in the mirror and began to sob. I couldn't believe what a grubby sight I was. I wasn't sunny at all; I was covered in dirty, grimy dog slobber from heel to toe.

Voices came from downstairs. It was Mr. Fuller and Nate.

"How many times do I have to tell you not to leave your basketball in the middle of the living room floor?" asked Mr. Fuller.

"Sorry, Dad! I just forgot," replied Nate.

"I nearly tripped over your things—again!" said Mr. Fuller, his footsteps coming upstairs.

UH-OH! I thought.

I tightened up my arches hoping he would not come into the bathroom—but he did. He marched right in and spotted me sitting meekly in the middle of the floor.

"Nate! I found your other sneaker! I'll toss it down to you," said Mr. Fuller.
WHAT?
"Okay, Dad!" answered Nate.

Mr. Fuller did not have a gentle touch. I was sent spiraling down the stairs, bouncing on each step— CLUNK! CLUNK! CLUNK!—to the hard floor below, landing with a THUNK! *OUCH!*

I slowly opened my eyes to see if I was scuffed, and standing right in front of me was Max!

He had that eager look in his eyes again. Luckily, this time he didn't bother me at all. He just stared at me for a moment, panting and wagging his tail, and dashed outside as if he never saw me. A feeling of relief swept over me, but I longed to be back in the hall closet where I belonged. I wanted to be with my mom and dad again.

My wishful thinking came to a quick halt as I heard Nate head my way.

He picked me up. "Now I can practice."

PRACTICE? PRACTICE WHAT? I thought with horror.

"Dad, I'll be in the driveway shooting hoops if you need me!" called Nate.

NO! NOT HOOPS!

Nate sat down and began to stuff his smelly, oversized foot into my small insides.

IS IT TOO MUCH TO ASK FOR A CLEAN SOCK?

I felt my seams pulling, and I wondered if I would ever move again. Then Nate stood up.

OH NO! HE IS GOING TO WALK ON ME!

Sure enough, he began to walk outside.

"Hmmm…maybe I should warm up before practice," Nate thought aloud. "I know, I'll run today—I haven't gone running in awhile."

RUNNING? NO!

My protest went unheard, and Nate began to sprint—not run—out of his driveway and down the street. I thought for sure my rubber sole would melt as my treads struck the hot pavement. I vaguely recalled my parents mentioning how humans need to break in their footwear. This must be what they meant!

Nate turned the corner and stopped.

"Hey, Matt!" he called in the window at his friend's house. "Maaaaattttttt!"

A boy about Nate's age came to the door.

"Nate, buddy, what's up?" said Matt.

"Want to shoot some hoops?" asked Nate.

"I was about to go swimming. Wanna swim instead?" invited Matt.

"Sure! Let's go!" replied Nate, and he walked to Matt's backyard to the swimming pool.

PHEW! I was off the hook.

Nate began to untie my laces.

"Where did you get those sneakers?" Matt asked. "They are the coolest things I've ever seen! A little muddy though."

COOL? HUH, ME?

"Thanks! They're new," laughed Nate. "But actually I have no idea how they got so dirty so fast."

He pulled me off and placed me atop a stone wall, then jumped into the pool, cannonball-style.

SWIMMING! NOW THERE'S A SPORT I CAN GET BEHIND, I thought as I kicked back, soaking in the sun.

But before I even had a chance to really relax, Josh appeared from out of the bushes by the stone wall. I had been warned about Josh. He's the neighborhood prankster, and I knew he'd be up to something. Josh tiptoed over to the wall quietly so that Nate and Matt couldn't hear him and prepared to reach down and snatch me. I was shaking in my boots.

It was then that, out of the corner of my eye, I noticed Max. He had been following us! He trotted into Matt's yard, looked around, immediately spotted Josh and began to charge toward him. Josh gasped, his plan foiled, and ran back through the bushes and into a neighboring yard.

MAX! MY HERO!

Max then picked me up, wagging his tail and galloped out of the yard. He ran with me rapidly down the street, around the corner and back into the Fuller home. We met Mr. Fuller in the kitchen as he was making lunch.

"Max! What are you doing with Nate's sneaker?" asked Mr. Fuller, laughing. He gently wrangled me free from Max's mouth, opened the hall closet and tossed me in.

HOORAY! HOME!

My parents saw me soaring in. Dad stretched out his tongue and caught me on the rebound.

"Son, you're back! How was your first big adventure?" my dad asked anxiously.

My mom gave me a giant, warm lace hug, awaiting my answer.

"I've
only been
gone one day," I
replied, breathless and
weary yet happy to be back.
"But if every day is like this, I might just
lose my sole."